THOMAS
THE TANK ENGINE

Favourite Stories from
the Railway Series

The Rev. W. Awdry

DEAN

This edition published in Great Britain in 2000 by Dean,
an imprint of Egmont Children's Books Limited, a division of
Egmont Holding Limited, 239 Kensington High Street, London W8 6SA
Thomas the Tank Engine first published in Great Britain in 1946
Tank Engine Thomas Again first published in Great Britain in 1949
Henry the Green Engine first published in Great Britain in 1951
Toby the Tram Engine first published in Great Britain in 1952
Gordon the Big Engine first published in Great Britain in 1953
The Eight Famous Engines first published in Great Britain in 1957

THE BRITT ALLCROFT COMPANY

Britt Allcroft's Thomas the Tank Engine & Friends
based on The Railway Series
by The Rev W Awdry
© Britt Allcroft (Thomas) LLC 2000
All underlying rights worldwide Britt Allcroft (Thomas) LLC
THE BRITT ALLCROFT COMPANY is a trademark of The Britt Allcroft Company plc
Afterword text © Brian Sibley 1996
This edition © Egmont Children's Books Limited 2000

ISBN 0 603 56015 6

3 5 7 9 10 8 6 4 2

Printed in Spain

 **Contents**

Thomas the Tank Engine

THE REV. W. AWDRY

Dear Christopher,

Here is your friend Thomas the Tank Engine.
He wanted to come out of his station yard and see the
world. These stories tell you how he did it.

I hope you will like them because you helped me to
make them.

Your Loving Daddy

Thomas and Gordon

THOMAS was a tank engine who lived at a Big Station. He had six small wheels, a short stumpy funnel, a short stumpy boiler, and a short stumpy dome.

He was a fussy little engine, always pulling coaches about. He pulled them to the station ready for the big engines to take out on long journeys; and when trains came in, and the people had got out, he would pull the empty coaches away, so that the big engines could go and rest.

He was a cheeky little engine, too. He thought no engine worked as hard as he did. So he used to play tricks on them. He liked best of all to come quietly beside a big engine dozing on a siding and make him jump.

"Peep, peep, peep, pip, peep! Wake up, lazybones!" he would whistle, "why don't you work hard like me?"

Then he would laugh rudely and run away to find some more coaches.

One day Gordon was resting on a siding. He was very tired. The big Express he always pulled had been late, and he had had to run as fast as he could to make up for lost time.

He was just going to sleep when Thomas came up in his cheeky way.

"Wake up, lazybones," he whistled, "do some hard work for a change – you can't catch me!" and he ran off laughing.

Instead of going to sleep again, Gordon thought how he could pay Thomas out.

One morning Thomas wouldn't wake up. His Driver and Fireman couldn't make him start. His fire went out and there was not enough steam.

It was nearly time for the Express. The people were waiting, but the coaches weren't ready.

At last Thomas started. "Oh, dear! Oh, dear!" he yawned.

"Come on," said the coaches. "Hurry up." Thomas gave them a rude bump, and started for the station.

"Don't stop dawdling, don't stop dawdling," he grumbled.

"Where have you been? Where have you been?" asked the coaches crossly. Thomas fussed into the station where Gordon was waiting.

"Poop, poop, poop. Hurry up, you," said Gordon crossly.

"Peep, pip, peep. Hurry yourself," said cheeky Thomas.

"Yes," said Gordon, "I will," and almost before the coaches had stopped moving Gordon came out of his siding and was coupled to the train.

"Poop, poop," he whistled. "Get in quickly, please." So the people got in quickly, the signal went down, the clock struck the

hour, the guard waved his green flag, and Gordon was ready to start.

Thomas usually pushed behind the big trains to help them start. But he was always uncoupled first, so that when the train was running nicely he could stop and go back.

This time he was late, and Gordon started so quickly that they forgot to uncouple Thomas.

"Poop, poop," said Gordon.

"Peep, peep, peep," whistled Thomas.

"Come on! Come on!" puffed Gordon to the coaches.

"Pull harder! Pull harder!" puffed Thomas to Gordon.

The heavy train slowly began to move out of the station.

The train went faster and faster; too fast for Thomas. He wanted to stop but he couldn't.

"Peep! Peep! Stop! Stop!" he whistled.

"Hurry, hurry, hurry," laughed Gordon in front.

"You can't get away. You can't get away," laughed the coaches.

Poor Thomas was going faster than he had ever gone before. He was out of breath and his wheels hurt him, but he had to go on.

"I shall never be the same again," he thought sadly, "My wheels will be quite worn out."

At last they stopped at a station. Everyone laughed to see Thomas puffing and panting behind.

They uncoupled him, put him on to a turntable and then he ran on a siding out of the way.

"Well, little Thomas," chuckled Gordon as he passed, "now you know what hard work means, don't you?"

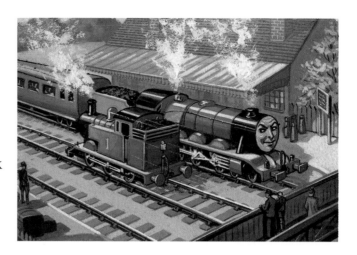

Poor Thomas couldn't answer, he had no breath. He just puffed slowly away to rest, and had a long, long drink.

He went home very slowly and was careful afterwards never to be cheeky to Gordon again.

Thomas' Train

THOMAS often grumbled because he was not allowed to pull passenger trains.

The other engines laughed. "You're too impatient," they said. "You'd be sure to leave something behind!"

"Rubbish," said Thomas, crossly. "You just wait, I'll show you."

One night he and Henry were alone. Henry was ill. The men worked hard, but he didn't get better.

Now Henry usually pulled the first train in the morning, and Thomas had to get his coaches ready.

"If Henry is ill," he thought, "perhaps I shall pull his train."

Thomas ran to find the coaches.

"Come *along*. Come *along*," he fussed.

"There's plenty of time, there's plenty of time," grumbled the coaches.

He took them to the platform, and wanted to run round in front at once. But his Driver wouldn't let him.

"Don't be impatient, Thomas," he said.

So Thomas waited and waited. The people got in, the Guard and Stationmaster walked up and down, the porters banged the doors, and still Henry didn't come.

Thomas got more and more excited every minute.

The Fat Director came out of his office to see what was the matter, and the Guard and the Stationmaster told him about Henry.

"Find another engine," he ordered.

"There's only Thomas," they said.

"You'll have to do it then, Thomas. Be quick now!"

So Thomas ran round to the front and backed down on the coaches ready to start.

"Don't be impatient," said his Driver. "Wait till everything is ready."

But Thomas was too excited to listen to a word he said.

What happened then no one knows. Perhaps they forgot to couple Thomas to the train; perhaps Thomas was too impatient to wait till they were ready; or perhaps his Driver pulled the lever by mistake.

Anyhow, Thomas started. People shouted and waved at him but he didn't stop.

"They're waving because I'm such a splendid engine," he thought importantly. "Henry says it's hard to pull trains, but *I* think it's easy."

"Hurry! Hurry! Hurry!" he puffed, pretending to be like Gordon.

As he passed the first signal box, he saw the men leaning out waving and shouting.

"They're pleased to see me," he thought. "They've never seen *me* pulling a train before – it's nice of them to wave," and he whistled, "Peep, peep, thank you," and hurried on.

But he came to a signal at "Danger".

"Bother!" he thought. "I must stop, and I was going so nicely, too. What a

nuisance signals are!" And he blew an angry "Peep, peep" on his whistle.

One of the Signalmen ran up. "Hullo, Thomas!" he said. "What are you doing here?"

"I'm pulling a train," said Thomas proudly. "Can't you *see?*"

"Where are your coaches, then?"

Thomas looked back. "Why bless me," he said, "if we haven't left them behind!"

"Yes," said the Signalman, "you'd better go back quickly and fetch them."

Poor Thomas was so sad he nearly cried.

"Cheer up!" said his Driver. "Let's go back quickly, and try again."

At the station all the passengers were talking at once. They were telling the Fat Director, the Stationmaster and the Guard what a bad railway it was.

But when Thomas came back and they saw how sad he was, they couldn't be cross. So they coupled him to the train, and this time he *really* pulled it.

But for a long time afterwards the other engines laughed at Thomas, and said:

"Look, there's Thomas, who wanted to pull a train, but forgot about the coaches!"

Thomas and the Trucks

THOMAS used to grumble in the Shed at night.

"I'm tired of pushing coaches, I want to see the world."

The others didn't take much notice, for Thomas was a little engine with a long tongue.

But one night, Edward came to the shed. He was a kind little engine, and felt sorry for Thomas.

"I've got some trucks to take home tomorrow," he told him. "If you take them instead, I'll push coaches in the Yard."

"Thank you," said Thomas, "that will be nice."

So they asked their Drivers next morning, and when they said "Yes,"

Thomas ran happily to find the trucks.

Now trucks are silly and noisy. They talk a lot and don't attend to what they are doing. They don't listen to their engine, and when he stops they bump into each other screaming.

"Oh! Oh! Oh! Oh! Whatever is happening?"

And, I'm sorry to say, they play tricks on an engine who is not used to them.

Edward knew all about trucks. He warned Thomas to be careful, but Thomas was too excited to listen.

The shunter fastened the coupling, and, when the signal dropped, Thomas was ready.

The Guard blew his whistle. "Peep! Peep!" answered Thomas and started off.

But the trucks weren't ready.

"Oh! Oh! Oh! Oh!" they screamed as their couplings tightened. "Wait, Thomas, wait." But Thomas wouldn't wait.

"Come — on; come — on," he puffed, and the trucks grumbled slowly out of the siding on to the main line.

Thomas was happy. "Come along. Come along," he puffed.

"All — right! — don't — fuss — all — right! — don't fuss," grumbled the trucks. They clattered through stations, and rumbled over bridges.

Thomas whistled "Peep! Peep!" and they rushed through the tunnel in which Henry had been shut up.

Then they came to the top of the hill where Gordon had stuck.

"Steady now, steady," warned the driver, and he shut off steam, and began to put on the brakes.

"We're stopping, we're stopping," called Thomas.

"No! No! No! No!" answered the trucks, and

bumped into each other. "Go — on! — go — on!" and before his driver could stop them, they had pushed Thomas down the hill, and were rattling and laughing behind him.

Poor Thomas tried hard to stop them from making him go too fast.

"Stop pushing, stop pushing," he hissed, but the trucks would not stop.

"Go — on! — go — on!" they giggled in their silly way.

He was glad when they got to the bottom. Then he saw in front the place where they had to stop.

"Oh, dear! What shall I do?"

They rattled through the station, and luckily the line was clear as they swerved into the goods yard.

"Oo —————— ooh e —————— r," groaned Thomas, as his brakes held fast and he skidded along the rails.

"I must stop," and he shut his eyes tight.

When he opened them he saw he had stopped just in front of the buffers, and there watching him was ———

The Fat Director!

"What are *you* doing here, Thomas?" he asked sternly.

"I've brought Edward's trucks," Thomas answered.

"Why did you come so fast?"

"I didn't mean to, I was *pushed*," said Thomas sadly.

"Haven't you pulled trucks before?"

"No."

"Then you've a lot to learn about trucks, little Thomas.

They are silly things and must be kept in their place. After pushing them about here for a few weeks you'll know almost as much about them as Edward. Then you'll be a Really Useful Engine."

Thomas and the Breakdown Train

EVERY day the Fat Director came to the station to catch his train, and he always said "Hullo" to Thomas.

There were lots of trucks in the Yard – different ones came in every day – and Thomas had to push and pull them into their right places.

He worked hard – he knew now that he wasn't so clever as he had thought. Besides, the Fat Director had been kind to him and he wanted to learn all about trucks so as to be a Really Useful Engine.

But on a siding by themselves were some trucks that Thomas was told he "mustn't touch".

There was a small coach, some flat trucks, and two queer things his Driver called cranes.

"That's the breakdown train," he said. "When there's an accident, the workmen get into the coach, and the engine takes them quickly to help the hurt people, and to clear and mend the line. The cranes are for lifting heavy things like engines, and coaches, and trucks."

One day, Thomas was in the Yard, when he heard an engine whistling "Help! Help!" and a goods train came rushing through much too fast.

The engine (a new one called James) was frightened. His brake blocks were on fire, and smoke and sparks streamed out on each side.

"They're *pushing* me! They're *pushing* me!" he panted.

"On! On! On! On!" laughed the trucks; and still whistling "Help! Help!"

poor James disappeared under a bridge.

"I'd like to teach those trucks a lesson," said Thomas the Tank Engine.

Presently a bell rang in the signal box, and a man came running, "James is off the line – the breakdown train – quickly," he shouted.

So Thomas was coupled on, the workmen jumped into their coach, and off they went.

Thomas worked his hardest. "Hurry! Hurry! Hurry!" he puffed, and this time he wasn't pretending to be like Gordon, he really meant it.

"Bother those trucks and their tricks," he thought, "I hope poor James isn't hurt."

They found James and the trucks at a bend in the line. The brake van and the last few trucks were on the rails, but the front ones were piled in a heap; James was in a field with a cow looking at him, and his Driver and Fireman were feeling him all over to see if he was hurt.

"Never mind, James," they said. "It wasn't your fault, it was those wooden brakes they gave you. We always said they were

no good."

Thomas pushed the breakdown train alongside. Then he pulled the unhurt trucks out of the way.

"Oh —— dear! — oh — dear!" they groaned.

"Serves you right. Serves you right," puffed Thomas crossly.

When the men put other trucks on the line he pulled them away, too. He was hard at work puffing backwards and forwards all the afternoon.

"This'll teach you a lesson, this'll teach you a lesson," he told the trucks, and they answered "Yes — it — will — yes — it — will," in a sad, groany, creaky, sort of voice.

They left the broken trucks and mended the line. Then with two cranes they put James back on the rails. He tried to move but he couldn't, so Thomas helped him back to the Shed.

The Fat Director was waiting anxiously for them.

"Well, Thomas," he said kindly, "I've heard all about it, and I'm very pleased with you. You're a Really Useful Engine.

"James shall have some proper brakes and a new coat of paint, and you —————— shall have a Branch Line all to yourself."

"Oh, Sir!" said Thomas, happily.

Now Thomas is as happy as can be. He has a branch line all to himself, and puffs proudly backwards and forwards with two coaches all day.

He is never lonely, because there is always some engine to talk to at the junction.

Edward and Henry stop quite often, and tell him the news. Gordon is always in a hurry and does not stop; but he never forgets to say "Poop, poop" to little Thomas, and Thomas always whistles "Peep, peep" in return.

— 24 —

THE RAILWAY SERIES NO. 4

Tank Engine Thomas Again

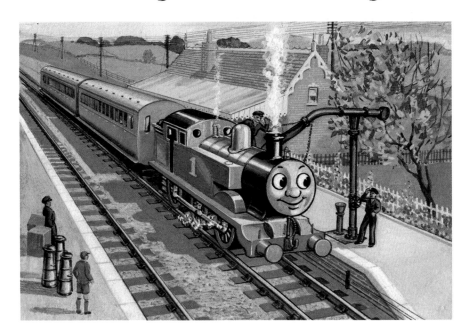

THE REV. W. AWDRY

with illustrations by

C. REGINALD DALBY

DEAR FRIENDS,

Here is news from Thomas' branch line. It is clearly no ordinary line, and life on it is far from dull.

Thomas asks me to say that, if you are ever in the Region, you must be sure to visit him and travel on his line. "They will have never seen anything like it," he says proudly.

I know I haven't!

THE AUTHOR

Thomas and the Guard

THOMAS the Tank Engine is very proud of his branch line. He thinks it is the most important part of the whole railway.

He has two coaches. They are old, and need new paint, but he loves them very much. He calls them Annie and Clarabel. Annie can only take passengers, but Clarabel can take passengers, luggage and the Guard.

As they run backwards and forwards along the line, Thomas sings them little songs, and Annie and Clarabel sing too.

When Thomas starts from a station he sings, "Oh, come along! We're rather late. Oh, come along! We're rather late." And the coaches sing, "We're coming along, we're coming along."

They don't mind what Thomas says to them because they know he is trying to please the Fat Controller; and they know, too, that if Thomas is cross, he is not cross with them.

He is cross with the engines on the Main Line who have made him late.

One day they had to wait for Henry's train. It was late. Thomas was getting crosser and crosser. "How can I run my line properly if Henry is always late? He doesn't realize that the Fat Controller depends on ME," and he whistled impatiently.

At last Henry came.

TANK ENGINE THOMAS AGAIN

"Where have you been, lazybones?" asked Thomas crossly.

"Oh dear, my system is out of order; no one understands my case. You don't know what I suffer," moaned Henry.

"Rubbish!" said Thomas, "you're too fat; you need exercise!"

Lots of people with piles of luggage got out of Henry's train, and they all climbed into Annie and Clarabel. Thomas had to wait till they were ready. At last the Guard blew his whistle, and Thomas started at once.

The Guard turned round to jump into his van, tripped over an old lady's umbrella, and fell flat on his face.

By the time he had picked himself up, Thomas and Annie and Clarabel were steaming out of the station.

"Come along! Come along!" puffed Thomas, but Clarabel didn't want to come. "I've lost my nice Guard, I've lost my nice Guard," she sobbed. Annie tried to tell Thomas "We haven't a Guard, we haven't a Guard," but he was hurrying, and wouldn't listen.

— 27 —

"Oh, come along! Oh, come along!" he puffed impatiently.

Annie and Clarabel tried to put on their brakes, but they couldn't without the Guard.

"Where is our Guard? Where is our Guard?" they cried. Thomas didn't stop till they came to a signal.

"Bother that signal!" said Thomas. "What's the matter?"

"I don't know," said his Driver. "The Guard will tell us in a minute." They waited and waited, but the Guard didn't come.

"Peep peep peep peep! Where is the Guard?" whistled Thomas.

"We've left him behind," sobbed Annie and Clarabel together. The Driver, the Fireman and the passengers looked, and there was the Guard running as fast as he could along the line, with his flags in one hand and his whistle in the other.

Everybody cheered him. He was very hot, so he sat down and had a drink and told them all about it.

"I'm very sorry, Mr Guard," said Thomas.

"It wasn't your fault, Thomas; it was the old lady's umbrella. Look, the signal is down; let's make up for lost time."

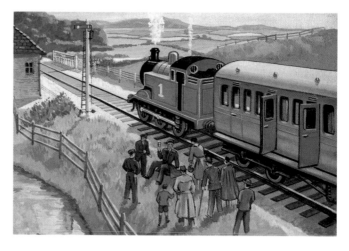

Annie and Clarabel were so pleased to have their Guard again, that they sang, "As fast as you like, as fast as you like!" to Thomas, all the way, and they reached the end of the line quicker than ever before.

Thomas goes Fishing

THOMAS' branch line had a station by a river. As he rumbled over the bridge, he would see people fishing. Sometimes they stood quietly by their lines; sometimes they were actually jerking fish out of the water.

Thomas often wanted to stay and watch, but his Driver said, "No! what would the Fat Controller say if we were late?"

Thomas thought it would be lovely to stop by the river. "I should like to go fishing," he said to himself longingly.

Every time he met another engine he would say "I want to fish." They all answered "Engines don't go fishing."

"Silly stick-in-the-muds!" he would snort impatiently.

Thomas generally had to take in water at the station by the river. One day he stopped as usual, and his Fireman put the pipe from the water tower in his tank. Then he turned the tap, but it was out of order and no water came.

"Bother!" said Thomas, "I am thirsty." "Never mind," said his Driver, "we'll get some water from the river."

They found a bucket and some rope, and went to the bridge, then the Driver let the bucket down to the water.

The bucket was old, and had five holes, so they had to fill it, pull it up, and empty it into Thomas' tank as quickly as they could.

"There's a hole in my bucket, dear Liza, dear Liza," sang the Fireman.

"Never mind about Liza," said the Driver, "you empty that bucket, before you spill the water over me!"

They finished at last. "That's good! That's good!" puffed Thomas as he started, and Annie and Clarabel ran happily behind.

They puffed along the valley, and were in the tunnel when Thomas began to feel a pain in his boiler, while steam hissed from his safety valve in an alarming way.

"There's too much steam," said his Driver, and his Fireman opened the tap in the feed pipe, to let more water into the boiler, but none came.

"Oh, dear," groaned Thomas, "I'm going to burst! I'm going to burst!"

They damped down his fire, and struggled on.

"I've got such a pain, I've got such a pain," Thomas hissed.

Just outside the last station they stopped, uncoupled Annie and Clarabel and ran Thomas,

who was still hissing fit to burst, on a siding right out of the way.

Then while the Guard telephoned for an Engine Inspector, and the Fireman was putting out the fire, the Driver wrote notices in large letters which he hung on Thomas in front and behind, "DANGER! KEEP AWAY."

Soon the Inspector and the Fat Controller arrived. "Cheer up, Thomas!" they said. "We'll soon put you right."

The Driver told them what had happened. "So the feed pipe is blocked," said the Inspector. "I'll just look in the tanks."

He climbed up and peered in, then he came down. "Excuse

me, Sir," he said to the Fat Controller, "please look in the tank and tell me what you see."

"Certainly, Inspector." He clambered up, looked in and nearly fell off in surprise.

"Inspector," he whispered, "can *you* see *fish*?"

"Gracious goodness me!" said the Fat Controller, "how did the fish get there, Driver?"

Thomas' Driver scratched his head, "We must have fished them from the river," and he told them about the bucket.

The Fat Controller laughed, "Well, Thomas, so you and your Driver have been fishing, but fish don't suit you, and we must get them out."

So the Driver and the Fireman fetched rods and nets, and they all took turns at fishing in Thomas' tank, while the Fat Controller told them how to do it.

When they had caught all the fish, the Stationmaster gave them some potatoes, the Driver borrowed a frying-pan, while the Fireman made a fire beside the line and did the cooking.

Then they all had a lovely picnic supper of fish and chips.

"That was good," said the Fat Controller as he finished his share, "but fish don't suit you, Thomas, so you mustn't do it again."

"No, Sir, I won't," said Thomas sadly, "engines don't go fishing, it's too uncomfortable."

Thomas, Terence and the Snow

AUTUMN was changing the leaves from green to brown. The fields were changing too, from yellow stubble to brown earth.

As Thomas puffed along, he heard the "chug chug chug" of a tractor at work.

One day, stopping for a signal, he saw the tractor close by.

"Hullo!" said the tractor, "I'm Terence; I'm ploughing."

"I'm Thomas; I'm pulling a train. What ugly wheels you've got."

"They're not ugly, they're caterpillars," said Terence. "I can go anywhere; *I* don't need rails."

"I don't want to go anywhere," said Thomas huffily, "I like my rails, thank you!"

Thomas often saw Terence working, but though he whistled, Terence never answered.

Winter came, and with it dark heavy clouds full of snow.

"I don't like it," said Thomas' Driver. "A heavy fall is coming. I hope it doesn't stop us."

"Pooh!" said Thomas, seeing the snow melt on the rails, "soft stuff, nothing to it!" And he puffed on feeling cold, but confident.

They finished their journey safely; but the country was covered, and the rails were two dark lines standing out in the white snow.

"You'll need your Snow Plough for the next journey, Thomas," said his Driver.

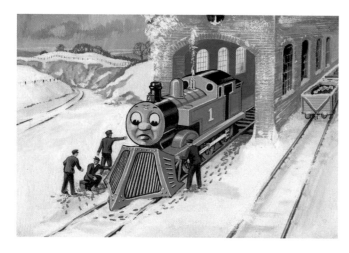

"Pooh! Snow is silly soft stuff – it won't stop me."

"Listen to me," his Driver replied, "we are going to fix your Snow Plough on, and I want no nonsense, please."

The Snow Plough was heavy and uncomfortable and made Thomas cross. He shook it, and he banged it and when they got back it was so damaged that the Driver had to take it off.

"You're a very naughty engine," said his Driver, as he shut the shed door that night.

Next morning, both Driver and Fireman came early and worked hard to mend the Snow Plough; but they couldn't make it fit properly.

It was time for the first train. Thomas was pleased, "I shan't have to wear it, I shan't have to wear it," he puffed to Annie and Clarabel.

"I hope it's all right, I hope it's all right," they whispered anxiously to each other.

The Driver was anxious, too. "It's not bad here," he said to the Fireman, "but it's sure to be deep in the valley."

It was snowing again when Thomas started, but the rails were not covered.

"Silly soft stuff! Silly soft stuff!" he puffed. "I didn't need that stupid old thing yesterday; I shan't today. Snow can't stop me," and he rushed into the tunnel, thinking how clever he was.

At the other end he saw a heap of snow fallen from the sides of the cutting.

"Silly old snow," said Thomas, and charged it.

"Cinders and ashes!" said Thomas, "I'm stuck!" – and he was!

"Back! Thomas, back!" said his Driver. Thomas tried, but his wheels spun, and he couldn't move.

More snow fell and piled up round him.

The Guard went back for help, while the Driver, Fireman and passengers tried to dig the snow away; but, as fast as they dug, more snow slipped down until Thomas was nearly buried.

"Oh, my wheels and coupling rods!" said Thomas sadly, "I shall have to stop here till I'm frozen. What a silly

engine I am," and Thomas began to cry.

At last, a tooting in the distance told them a bus had come for the passengers.

Then Terence chugged through the tunnel.

He pulled the empty coaches away, and came back for Thomas. Thomas' wheels were clear, but still spun helplessly when he tried to move.

Terence tugged and slipped,

and slipped and tugged, and at last dragged Thomas into the tunnel.

"Thank you, Terence, your caterpillars are splendid," said Thomas gratefully.

"I hope you'll be sensible now, Thomas," said his Driver severely.

"I'll try," said Thomas, as he puffed home.

Thomas and Bertie

ONE day Thomas was waiting at the junction, when a bus came into the Yard.

"Hullo!" said Thomas, "who are you?"

"I'm Bertie, who are you?"

"I'm Thomas; I run this line."

"So you're Thomas. Ah – I remember now, you stuck in the snow, I took your passengers and Terence pulled you out. I've come to help you with your passengers today."

"Help me!" said Thomas crossly, going bluer than ever and letting off steam. "I can go faster than you."

"You can't."

"I can."

"I'll race you," said Bertie. Their Drivers agreed. The Stationmaster said, "Are you ready? – Go!" and they were off.

Thomas never could go fast at first, and Bertie drew in front. Thomas was running well but he did not hurry.

"Why don't you go fast? Why don't you go fast?" called Annie and Clarabel anxiously.

"Wait and see, wait and see," hissed Thomas.

"He's a long way ahead, a long way ahead," they wailed, but Thomas didn't mind. He remembered the level crossing.

There was Bertie fuming at the gates while they sailed gaily through.

"Goodbye, Bertie," called Thomas.

The road left the railway and went through a village, so they couldn't see Bertie.

They stopped at the station. "Peep pip peep! Quickly, please!" called Thomas. Everybody got out quickly, the Guard whistled and off they went.

"Come along! Come along!" sang Thomas.

"We're coming along! We're coming along!" sang Annie and Clarabel.

"Hurry! Hurry! Hurry!" panted Thomas, looking straight ahead.

Then he whistled shrilly in horror, for Bertie was crossing the bridge over the railway, tooting triumphantly on his horn!

"Oh, deary me! Oh, deary me!" groaned Thomas.

"He's a long way in front, a long way in front," wailed Annie and Clarabel.

"Steady, Thomas," said his Driver, "we'll beat Bertie yet."

"We'll beat Bertie yet; we'll beat Bertie yet," echoed Annie and Clarabel.

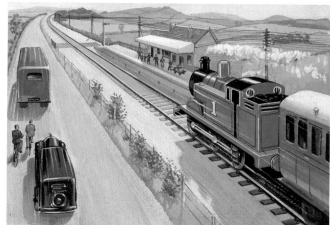

"We'll do it; we'll do it," panted Thomas bravely. "Oh, bother, there's a station."

As he stopped, he heard a toot.

"Goodbye, Thomas, you must be tired. Sorry I can't stop, we buses have to work you know. Goodbye!"

The next station was by the river. They got there quickly, but the signal was up.

"Oh, dear," thought Thomas, "we've lost!"

But he felt better after a drink. Then James rattled through with a goods train, and the signal dropped, showing the line was clear.

"Hurrah, we're off! Hurrah, we're off!" puffed Thomas gaily.

As they rumbled over the bridge they heard an impatient "Toot, Toot," and there was Bertie waiting at the red light, while cars and lorries crossed the narrow bridge in the opposite direction.

Road and railway ran up the valley side by side, a stream tumbling between.

Thomas had not crossed the bridge when Bertie started with a roar, and soon shot ahead. Excited passengers in train and bus cheered and shouted across the valley. Now Thomas reached his full speed and foot by foot, yard by yard

he gained, till they were running level. Bertie tried hard, but Thomas was too fast; slowly but surely he drew ahead, till whistling triumphantly he plunged into the tunnel, leaving Bertie toiling far behind.

"I've done it! I've done it," panted Thomas in the tunnel.

"We've done it, hooray! We've done it, hooray!" chanted

Annie and Clarabel; and whistling proudly, they whooooshed out of the tunnel into the last station.

The passengers gave Thomas "three cheers" and told the Stationmaster and the porters all about the race. When Bertie came in they gave him "three cheers" too.

"Well done, Thomas," said Bertie. "That was fun, but to beat you over that hill I should have to grow wings and be an aeroplane."

Thomas and Bertie now keep each other very busy. Bertie finds people in the villages who want to go by train, and takes them to Thomas; while Thomas brings people to the station for Bertie to take home.

They often talk about their race. But Bertie's passengers don't like being bounced like peas in a frying-pan! And the Fat Controller has warned Thomas about what happens to engines who race at dangerous speeds.

So although (between you and me) they would like to have another race, I don't think they ever will.

THE RAILWAY SERIES NO. 6

Henry the Green Engine

THE REV. W. AWDRY

with illustrations by

C. REGINALD DALBY

DEAR FRIENDS,

Here is more news from the Region. All the engines now have numbers as well as names; you will see them in the pictures. They are as follows: THOMAS 1, EDWARD 2, HENRY 3, GORDON 4, JAMES 5, PERCY 6.

Then I expect you were sorry for Henry who was often ill and unable to work. He gave Sir Topham Hatt (who is, of course, our Fat Controller) a lot of worry. Now Henry has a new shape and is ready for anything. These stories tell you all about it.

THE AUTHOR

Coal

"I SUFFER dreadfully, and no one cares."

"Rubbish, Henry," snorted James, "you don't work hard enough."

Henry was bigger than James, but smaller than Gordon. Sometimes he could pull trains; sometimes he had no strength at all.

The Fat Controller spoke to him too. "You are too expensive, Henry. You have had lots of new parts and new paint too, but they've done you no good. If we can't make you better, we must get another engine instead of you."

This made Henry, his Driver, and his Fireman very sad.

The Fat Controller was waiting when Henry came to the platform. He had taken off his hat and coat, and put on overalls.

He climbed to the footplate and Henry started.

"Henry is a 'bad steamer'," said the Fireman. "I build up his fire, but it doesn't give enough heat."

Henry tried very hard, but it was no good. He had not enough steam, and they stopped outside Edward's station.

"Oh dear!" thought Henry sadly, "I shall have to go away."

Edward took charge of the train. Henry stopped behind.

"What do you think is wrong, Fireman?" asked the Fat Controller.

The Fireman mopped his face. "Excuse me, Sir," he answered, "but the coal is wrong. We've had a poor lot lately, and today it's worse. The other engines can manage; they have big fireboxes. Henry's is small and can't make the heat. With Welsh coal he'd be a different engine."

"It's expensive," said the Fat Controller thoughtfully, "but Henry must have a fair chance. James shall go and fetch some."

When the Welsh coal came, Henry's Driver and Fireman were excited.

"Now we'll show them, Henry old fellow!" They carefully oiled all his joints and polished his brass till it shone like gold.

His fire had already been lit, so the Fireman "made it" carefully.

He put large lumps of coal like a wall round the outside. Then he covered the glowing middle part with smaller lumps.

"You're spoiling my fire," complained Henry.

"Wait and see," said the Fireman. "We'll have a roaring fire just when we want it."

He was right. When Henry reached the platform, the water was boiling nicely, and he had to let off steam, to show how

happy he was. He made such a noise that the Fat Controller came out to see him.

"How are you, Henry?"

"Pip peep peep!" whistled Henry, "I feel fine!"

"Have you a good fire, Driver?"

"Never better Sir, *and* plenty of steam."

"No record breaking," warned the Fat Controller, smiling. "Don't push him too hard."

"Henry won't need pushing, Sir; I'll have to hold him back."

Henry had a lovely day. He had never felt so well in his life. He wanted to go fast, but his Driver wouldn't let him. "Steady old fellow," he would say, "there's plenty of time."

They arrived early at the junction.

"Where have you been, lazybones?" asked Henry, when Thomas puffed in, "I can't wait

for dawdling tank engines like you! Goodbye!"

"Whoooosh!" said Thomas to Annie and Clarabel as Henry disappeared, "have you ever seen anything like it?"

Both Annie and Clarabel agreed that they never had.

The Flying Kipper

LOTS of ships use the harbour at the Big Station by the sea. The passenger ships have spotless paint and shining brass. Other ships, though smaller and dirtier, are important too. They take coal, machinery and other things abroad, and bring back meat, timber and things we need.

Fishing boats also come there. They unload their fish on the quay. Some of it is sent to shops in the town, and some goes in a special train to other places far away.

The railwaymen call this train "The Flying Kipper".

One winter evening Henry's Driver said: "We'll be out early tomorrow. We've got to take 'The Flying Kipper'."

"Don't tell Gordon," he whispered, "but I think if we pull the 'Kipper' nicely, the Fat Controller will let us pull the Express."

"Hurrah!" cried Henry, excited. "That will be lovely."

He was ready at 5 o'clock. There was snow and frost. Men hustled and shouted, loading the vans with crates of fish. The last door banged, the Guard showed his green lamp, and they were off.

"Come on! Come on! dontbesilly! — dontbesilly!" puffed Henry to the vans, as his wheels slipped on the icy rails.

The vans shuddered and groaned. "Trock, Trick, Trock, Trick; all right, all right," they answered grudgingly.

"That is better, that is better," puffed Henry more happily, as the train began to gather speed.

Thick clouds of smoke and steam poured from his funnel into the cold air; and when his Fireman put on more coal, the fire's light shone brightly on the snow around.

"Hurry, hurry, hurry," panted Henry.

They hooshed under bridges, and clattered through stations, green signal-lights showing as they passed.

They were going well, the light grew better and a yellow signal appeared ahead.

"Distant signal – up," thought Henry, "caution." His Driver, shutting off steam, prepared to stop, but the home signal was down. "All clear, Henry; away we go."

They couldn't know the points from the main line to a siding were frozen, and that that signal had been set at "danger." A fall of snow had forced it down.

A goods train waited in the siding to let "The Flying Kipper" pass. The Driver and Fireman were drinking cocoa in the brake van.

The Guard pulled out his watch. "The 'Kipper' is due," he said.

"Who cares?" said the Fireman. "This is good cocoa."

The Driver got up, "Come on Fireman, back to our engine."

"Hey!" the Fireman grumbled, "I haven't finished my cocoa yet."

A sudden crash – the brake van broke – the three men shot in the air like Jacks-in-the-box, and landed in the snow outside.

Henry's Driver and the Fireman jumped clear before the crash. The Fireman fell head first into a heap of snow. He kicked so hard that the Driver couldn't pull him out.

Henry sprawled on his side. He looked surprised. The goods train Fireman waved his empty mug.

"You clumsy great engine! The best cup of cocoa I've ever had, and you bump into me and spill it all!"

"Never mind your cocoa, Fireman," laughed his Driver, "run and telephone the breakdown gang."

The gang soon cleared the line, but they had hard work lifting Henry to the rails.

The Fat Controller came to see him.

"The signal was down, Sir," said Henry nervously.

"Cheer up, Henry! It wasn't your fault. Ice and snow caused the accident. I'm sending you to Crewe, a fine place for sick engines. They'll give you a new shape and a larger firebox. Then you'll feel a different engine, and won't need special coal any more. Won't that be nice?"

"Yes, Sir," said Henry doubtfully.

Henry liked being at Crewe, but was glad to come home.

A crowd of people waited to see him arrive in his new shape. He looked so splendid and strong that they gave him three cheers.

"Peep peep pippippeep! Thank you very much," he whistled happily.

I am sorry to say that a lot of little boys are often late for school because they wait to see Henry go by!

They often see him pulling the Express; and he does it so well that Gordon is jealous. But that is another story.

Gordon's Whistle

GORDON was cross.

"Why should Henry have a new shape?" he grumbled. "A shape good enough for ME is good enough for him. He goes gallivanting off to Crewe, leaving us to do his work. It's disgraceful!"

"And there's another thing. Henry whistles too much. No *respectable* engine ever whistles loudly at stations."

"It isn't wrong," said Gordon, "but we just don't do it."

Poor Henry didn't feel happy any more.

"Never mind," whispered Percy, "I'm glad you are home again; I like your whistling."

"Goodbye, Henry," called Gordon next morning as he left the Shed. "We are glad to have you with us again, but be sure and remember what I said about whistling."

Later on Henry took a slow train, and presently stopped at Edward's station.

"Hullo Henry," said

Edward, "you look splendid; I was pleased to hear your happy whistle yesterday."

"Thank you, Edward," smiled Henry . . . "Sh Sh! Can you hear something?"

Edward listened – far away, but getting louder and louder, was the sound of an engine's whistle.

"It sounds like Gordon," said Edward, "and it ought to be Gordon, but Gordon never whistles like that."

It *was* Gordon.

He came rushing down the hill at a tremendous rate. He didn't look at Henry, and he didn't look at Edward; he was purple in the boiler, and whistling fit to burst.

He screamed through the station and disappeared.

"Well!!!" said Edward, looking at Henry.

"It isn't wrong," chuckled Henry, "but we just don't do it," and he told Edward what Gordon had said.

Meanwhile Gordon screeched along the line. People came out of their houses, air-raid sirens started, five fire brigades got ready to go out, horses upset their carts, and old ladies dropped their parcels.

At a Big Station the noise was awful. Porters and passengers held their ears. The Fat Controller held his ears too; he gave a lot of orders, but no one could hear them, and Gordon went on whistling. At last he clambered into Gordon's cab.

"Take him away," he bellowed, "**AND STOP THAT NOISE!**"

Still whistling, Gordon puffed sadly away.

He whistled as he crossed the points; he whistled on the siding; he was still whistling as the last deafened passenger left the station.

Then two fitters climbed up and knocked his whistle valve into place ——

—— and there was SILENCE.

Gordon slunk into the Shed. He was glad it was empty.

The others came in later. "It isn't wrong," murmured Henry to no one in particular, "but we just don't do it."

No one mentioned whistles!

Percy and the Trousers

ON cold mornings Percy often saw workmen wearing scarves.

"My funnel's cold, my funnel's cold!" he would puff; "I want a scarf, I want a scarf."

"Rubbish, Percy," said Henry one day, "engines don't want scarves!"

"Engines with proper funnels do," said Percy in his cheeky way. "You've only got a small one!"

Henry snorted; he was proud of his short, neat funnel.

Just then a train came in and Percy, still puffing "I want a scarf, I want a scarf," went to take the coaches to their siding.

His Driver always shut off steam just outside the station, and Percy would try to surprise the coaches by coming in as quietly as he could.

Two porters were taking some luggage across the line. They had a big load and were walking backwards, to see that none fell off the trolley.

Percy arrived so quietly that the porters didn't hear him till the trolley was on the line. The porters jumped clear. The trolley disappeared with a crunch.

Boxes and bags burst in all directions.

"Oo —— ooh e —— r!" groaned Percy and stopped. Sticky streams of red and yellow jam trickled down his face. A top hat hung on his lamp-iron. Clothes, hats, boots, shoes, skirts and blouses stuck to his front. A pair of striped trousers coiled lovingly round his funnel. They were grey no longer!

This story is adapted from one told by Mr. C. Hamilton Ellis in *The Trains We Loved*. We gratefully acknowledge his permission to use it.

Angry passengers looked at their broken trunks. The Fat Controller seized the top hat.

"Mine!" he said crossly.

"Percy," he shouted, "look at this."

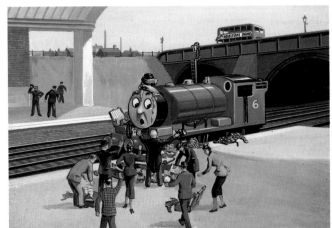

"Yes Sir, I am Sir," a muffled voice replied.

"My best trousers too!"

"Yes Sir, please Sir," said Percy nervously.

"I am very cross," said the Fat Controller. "We must pay the passengers for their spoilt clothes. My hat is dented, and my trousers are ruined, all because you *will* come into the station as if you were playing 'Grandmother's Steps' with the coaches."

The Driver unwound the trousers.

The Fat Controller waved them away.

"Percy wanted a scarf; he shall have my trousers for a scarf; they will keep him warm."

Percy wore them back to the Yard.

He doesn't like scarves now!

Henry's Sneeze

ONE lovely Saturday morning, Henry was puffing along. The sun shone, the fields were green, the birds sang; Henry had plenty of steam in his boiler, and he was feeling happy.

"I feel so well, I feel so well," he sang.

"Trickety trock, Trickety trock," hummed his coaches.

Henry saw some boys on a bridge.

"Peep! Peep! Hullo!" he whistled cheerfully.

"Peep! Peep! Peeeep!" he called the next moment. "Oh! Oh! Oooh!" For the boys didn't wave and take his number; they dropped stones on him instead.

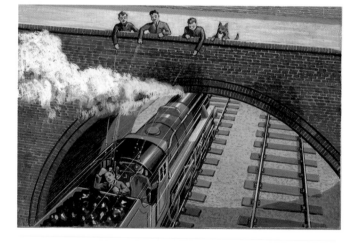

They were silly, stupid boys who thought it would be fun to drop stones down his funnel. Some of the stones hit Henry's boiler and spoilt his paint; one hit the Fireman on the head as he was shovelling coal, and others broke the carriage windows.

"It's a shame, it's a shame," hissed Henry.

"They've broken our glass, they've broken our glass," sobbed the coaches.

The Driver opened the first-aid box, bandaged the Fireman's head, and planned what he was going to do.

They stopped the train and the Guard asked if any passengers were hurt. No one was hurt, but everyone was cross. They saw the Fireman's bumped head, and told him what to do for it, and they looked at Henry's paint.

"Call the Police," they shouted angrily.

"No!" said the Driver, "leave it to Henry and me. We'll teach those lads a lesson."

"What will you do?" they asked.

"Can you keep a secret?"

"Yes, yes," they all said.

"Well then," said the Driver, "Henry is going to sneeze at them."

"What!" cried all the passengers.

The Driver laughed. "Henry draws air in through his fire, and puffs it out with smoke and steam. When he puffs hard, the air blows ashes from his fire into his smokebox, and 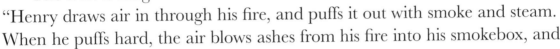 these ashes sometimes prevent him puffing properly.

"When your nose is blocked, you sometimes sneeze. If Henry's smoke box is blocked, I can make air and steam blow the ashes out through his funnel.

"We will do it at the bridge and startle those boys."

Henry puffed on to the terminus, where he had a rest. Then he took the train back. Lots of people were waiting at the station just before the bridge. They wanted to see what would happen.

"Henry has plenty of ashes," said the Driver. "Please keep all windows shut till we have passed the bridge. Henry is as excited as we are, aren't you old fellow?" and he patted Henry's boiler.

Henry didn't answer; he was feeling "stuffed up", but he winked at his Driver, like this.

The Guard's flag waved, his whistle blew, and they were off. Soon in the distance they saw the bridge. There were the boys, and they all had stones.

"Are you ready, Henry?" said his Driver. "Sneeze hard when I tell you."

"NOW!" he said, and turned the handle.

"Atisha Atisha Atishoooooh!"

Smoke and steam and ashes spouted from his funnel. They went all over the bridge, and all over the boys who ran away as black as soot.

"Well done, Henry," laughed his Driver, "they won't drop stones on engines again."

"Your coat is all black, but we'll rub you down and paint your scratches and you'll be as good as new tomorrow."

Henry has never again sneezed under a bridge. The Fat Controller doesn't like it. His smoke box is always cleaned in the Yard while he is resting.

He has now gone under more bridges than he can count; but from that day to this there have been no more boys with stones.

THE RAILWAY SERIES NO. 7

Toby the Tram Engine

THE REV. W. AWDRY

with illustrations by

C. REGINALD DALBY

DEAR FRIENDS,

Poor Thomas has been in trouble. So the Fat Controller asked Toby to come and help run the Branch Line. Thomas and Toby are very good friends.

Toby is a funny little engine with a queer shape. He works very hard and we are fond of him. We hope you will like him too.

THE AUTHOR

Toby and the Stout Gentleman

TOBY is a Tram Engine. He is short and sturdy. He has cow-catchers and side-plates, and doesn't look like a steam engine at all. He takes trucks from farms

and factories to the Main Line, and the big engines take them to London and elsewhere. His tramline runs along roads and through fields and villages. Toby rings his bell cheerfully to everyone he meets.

He has a coach called Henrietta, who has seen better days. She complains because she has few passengers. Toby is attached to Henrietta and always takes her with him.

"She might be useful one day," he says.

"It's not fair at all!" grumbles Henrietta as the buses roar past full of passengers. She remembers that she used to be full, and nine trucks would rattle behind her.

Now there are only three or four, for the farms and factories send their goods mostly by lorry.

Toby is always careful on the road. The cars, buses and lorries often have accidents. Toby hasn't had an accident for years, but the buses are crowded, and Henrietta is empty.

"I can't understand it," says Toby the tram engine.

People come to see Toby, but they come by bus. They stare at him. "Isn't he quaint!" they say, and laugh.

They make him so cross.

One day a car stopped close by, and a little boy jumped out. "Come on Bridget," he called to his sister, and together they ran across to Toby. Two ladies and a stout gentleman followed. The gentleman looked important, but nice.

The children ran back. "Come on grandfather, do look at this engine," and seizing his hands they almost dragged him along.

"That's a tram engine, Stephen," said the stout gentleman.

"Is it electric?" asked Bridget.

"Whoosh!" hissed Toby crossly.

"Sh Sh!" said her brother, "you've offended him."

"But trams *are* electric, aren't they?"

"They are mostly," the stout gentleman answered, "but this is a steam tram."

"May we go in it grandfather? Please!"
The Guard had begun to blow his whistle.

"Stop," said the stout gentleman, and raised his hand. The Guard, surprised, opened his mouth, and the whistle fell out.

While he was picking it up, they all scrambled into Henrietta.

"Hip Hip Hurray!" chanted Henrietta, and she rattled happily behind.

Toby did not sing. "Electric indeed! Electric indeed," he snorted. He was very hurt.

The stout gentleman and his family got out at the junction, but waited for Toby to take them back to their car.

"What is your name?" asked the stout gentleman.

"Toby, Sir."

"Thank you, Toby, for a very nice ride."

"Thank *you*, Sir," said Toby politely. He felt better now. "This gentleman," he thought, "is a gentleman who knows how to speak to engines."

The children came every day for a fortnight. Sometimes they rode with the Guard, sometimes in empty trucks, and on the last day of all the Driver invited them into his cab.

All were sorry when they had to go away.

Stephen and Bridget said "Thank you" to Toby, his Driver, his Fireman, and the Guard.

The stout gentleman gave them all a present.

"Peep pip pip peep," whistled Toby. "Come again soon."

"We will, we will," called the children, and they waved till Toby was out of sight.

The months passed. Toby had few trucks, and fewer passengers.

"Our last day, Toby," said his Driver sadly one morning. "The Manager says we must close tomorrow."

That day Henrietta had more passengers than she could manage. They rode in the trucks and crowded in the brake van, and the Guard hadn't enough tickets to go round.

The passengers joked and sang, but Toby and his Driver wished they wouldn't.

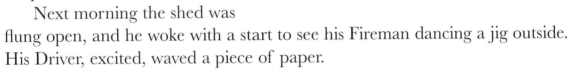

"Goodbye, Toby," said the passengers afterwards, "we are sorry your line is closing down."

"So am I," said Toby sadly.

The last passenger left the station, and Toby puffed slowly to his shed.

"Nobody wants me," he thought, and went unhappily to sleep.

Next morning the shed was flung open, and he woke with a start to see his Fireman dancing a jig outside. His Driver, excited, waved a piece of paper.

"Wake up, Toby," they shouted, "and listen to this; it's a letter from the stout gentleman."

Toby listened and . . .

But I mustn't tell you any more, or I should spoil the next story.

Thomas in Trouble

THERE is a line to a quarry at the end of Thomas' Branch; it goes for some distance along the road.

Thomas was always very careful here in case anyone was coming.

"Peep pip peep!" he whistled; then the people got out of the way, and he puffed slowly along with his trucks rumbling behind him.

Early one morning there was no one on the road, but a large policeman was sitting on the grass close to the line. He was shaking a stone from his boot.

Thomas liked policemen. He had been a great friend of the Constable who used to live in the village; but he had just retired.

Thomas expected that the new Constable would be friendly too.

"Peep peep," he whistled, "good morning."

The policeman jumped and dropped his boot. He scrambled up, and hopped round on one leg till he was facing Thomas.

Thomas was sorry to see that he didn't look friendly at all. He was red in the face and very cross.

The policeman wobbled about, trying to keep his balance.

"Disgraceful!" he spluttered. "I didn't sleep a wink last night, it was so quiet, and now engines come whistling suddenly behind me! My first day in the country too!"

He picked up his boot and hopped over to Thomas.

"I'm sorry, Sir," said Thomas, "I only said 'good morning'."

The policeman grunted, and, leaning against Thomas' buffer, he put his boot on.

He drew himself up and pointed to Thomas.

"Where's your cow-catcher?" he asked accusingly.

"But I don't catch cows, Sir!"

"Don't be funny!" snapped the policeman. He looked at Thomas' wheels. "No side plates either," and he wrote in his notebook.

"Engines going on Public Roads must have their wheels covered, and a cow-catcher in front. You haven't, so you are Dangerous to the Public."

"Rubbish!" said his Driver, "we've been along here hundreds of times and never had an accident."

"That makes it worse," the policeman answered. He wrote "regular lawbreaker" in his book.

Thomas puffed sadly away.

The Fat Controller was having breakfast. He was eating

toast and marmalade. He had the newspaper open in front of him, and his wife had just given him some more coffee.

The butler knocked and came in.

"Excuse me, Sir, you are wanted on the telephone."

"Bother that telephone!" said the Fat Controller.

"I'm sorry, my dear," he said a few minutes later, "Thomas is in trouble with the police, and I must go at once."

He gulped down his coffee and hurried from the room.

At the junction, Thomas' Driver told the Fat Controller what had happened.

"Dangerous to the Public indeed; we'll see about that!" and he climbed grimly into Annie the coach.

The policeman was on the platform at the other end. The Fat Controller spoke to him at once, and a crowd collected to listen.

Other policemen came to see what was happening and the Fat Controller argued with them too; but it was no good.

"The Law is the Law," they said, "and we can't change it."

The Fat Controller felt exhausted.

He mopped his face.

"I'm sorry Driver," he said, "it's no use arguing with policemen. We will have to make those cow-catcher things for Thomas, I suppose."

"Everyone will laugh, Sir," said Thomas sadly, "they'll say I look like a tram."

The Fat Controller stared, then he laughed.

"Well done, Thomas! Why didn't I think of it before? We want a tram engine! When I was on my holiday, I met a nice little engine called Toby. He hasn't enough work to do, and needs a change. I'll write to his Controller at once."

A few days later Toby arrived.

"That's a good engine," said the Fat Controller, "I see you've brought Henrietta."

"You don't mind, do you, Sir?" asked Toby anxiously. "The Stationmaster wanted to use her as a hen house, and that would never do."

"No, indeed," said the Fat Controller gravely, "we couldn't allow that."

Toby made the trucks behave even better than Thomas did.

At first Thomas was jealous, but he was so pleased when Toby rang his bell and made the policeman jump that they have been firm friends ever since.

Dirty Objects

TOBY and Henrietta take the workmen to the Quarry every morning. At the junction they often meet James.

Toby and Henrietta were shabby when they first came, and needed new paint. James was very rude. "Ugh! What *dirty* objects!" he would say.

At last Toby lost patience.

"James," he asked, "why are you red?"

"I am a splendid engine," answered James loftily, "ready for anything. You never see *my* paint dirty."

"Oh!" said Toby innocently, "that's why you once needed bootlaces; to be ready, I suppose."

James went redder than ever, and snorted off.

At the end of the line James left his coaches and got ready for his next train. It was a "slow goods", stopping at every station to pick up and set down trucks. James hated slow goods trains.

"Dirty trucks from dirty sidings! Ugh!" he grumbled.

Starting with only a few, he picked up more and more trucks at each station, till he had a long train. At first the trucks behaved well, but James bumped them so crossly that they determined to pay him out.

Presently, rumbling over the viaduct, they approached the top of Gordon's Hill. Heavy goods trains halt here to "pin down" their brakes. James had had an accident with trucks before, and should have remembered this.

"Wait, James, wait," said his Driver, but James wouldn't wait. He was too busy thinking what he would say to Toby when they next met.

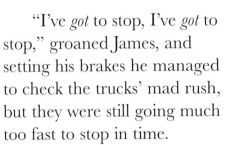

Too late he saw where he was, and tried to stop.

"Hurrah! Hurrah!" laughed the trucks, and banging their buffers they pushed him down the hill.

The Guard tightened his brakes until they screamed.

"On! On! On!" yelled the trucks.

"I've *got* to stop, I've *got* to stop," groaned James, and setting his brakes he managed to check the trucks' mad rush, but they were still going much too fast to stop in time.

Through the station they thundered, and lurched into the Yard.

James shut his eyes ———
There was a bursting crash, and something sticky splashed all over him. He had run into two tar wagons, and was black from smokebox to cab.

James was more dirty than hurt, but the tar wagons and some of the trucks were all to pieces. The breakdown train was in the Yard, and they soon tidied up the mess.

Toby and Percy were sent to help, and came as quickly as they could.

"Look here, Percy!" exclaimed Toby, "whatever is that dirty object?"

"That's James; didn't you know?"

"It's James' shape," said Toby thoughtfully, "but James is a splendid red

engine, and you never see *his* paint dirty."

James shut his eyes, and pretended he hadn't heard.

They cleared away the unhurt trucks, and helped James home.

The Fat Controller met them.

"Well done, Percy and Toby," he said.

He turned to James. "Fancy letting your trucks run away. I *am* surprised. You're not fit to be seen; you must be cleaned at once."

"Toby shall have a coat of paint – chocolate and blue I think."

"Please, Sir, can Henrietta have one too?"

"Certainly Toby," he smiled, "she shall have brown like Annie and Clarabel."

"Oh thank you, Sir! She will be pleased."

Toby ran home happily to tell her the news.

Mrs Kyndley's Christmas

IT was nearly Christmas. Annie and Clarabel were packed full of people and parcels.

Thomas was having very hard work.

"Come on! Come on!" he puffed.

"We're feeling *so* full!" grumbled the coaches.

Thomas looked at the hill ahead. "Can I do it? Can I do it?" he puffed anxiously.

Suddenly he saw a handkerchief waving from a cottage window. He felt better at once.

"Yes I can, yes I can," he puffed bravely. He pulled his hardest, and was soon through the tunnel and resting in the station.

"That was Mrs Kyndley who waved to you, Thomas," his Driver told him. "She has to stay in bed all day."

"Poor lady," said Thomas, "I am sorry for her."

Engines have heavy loads at Christmas time, but Thomas and Toby didn't mind the hard work when they saw Mrs Kyndley waving.

But then it began to rain. It rained for days and days.

Thomas didn't like it, nor did his Driver.

"Off we go Thomas!" he would say. "Pull hard and get home quickly; Mrs Kyndley won't wave today."

But whether she waved or not, they always whistled when they passed the little lonely cottage. Its white walls stood out against the dark background of the hills.

"Hello!" exclaimed Thomas' Fireman one day. "Look at that!"

The Driver came across the cab. "Something's wrong there," he said.

Hanging flapping and bedraggled from a window of the cottage was something that looked like a large red flag.

"Mrs Kyndley needs help I expect," said the Driver, and put on the brakes. Thomas gently stopped.

The Guard came squelching through the rain up to Thomas's cab, and the Driver pointed to the flag.

"See if a Doctor's on the train and ask him to go to the cottage; then walk back to the station and tell them we've stopped."

The Fireman went to see if the line was clear in front.

Two passengers left the train and climbed to the cottage. Then the Fireman returned.

"We'll back down to the station," said the Driver, "so that Thomas can get a good start."

"We shan't get up the hill," the Fireman answered. "Come and see what's happened!"

They walked along the line round the bend.

"Jiminy Christmas!" exclaimed the Driver, "go back to the train; I'm going to the cottage."

He found the Doctor with Mrs Kyndley.

"Silly of me to faint," she said.

"You saw the red dressing-gown? You're all safe?" asked Mrs Kyndley.

"Yes," smiled the Driver, "I've come to thank you. There was a landslide in the cutting, Doctor, and Mrs Kyndley saw it from her window and stopped us. She's saved our lives!"

"God bless you, ma'am," said the Driver, and tiptoed from the room.

They cleared the line by Christmas Day, and the sun shone as a special train puffed up from the junction.

First came Toby, then Thomas with Annie and Clarabel, and last of all, but very pleased at being allowed to come, was Henrietta.

The Fat Controller was there, and lots of other people who wanted to say "Thank you" to Mrs Kyndley.

"Peepeep, Peepeep! Happy Christmas!" whistled the engines as they reached the place.

The people got out and climbed to the cottage. Thomas and Toby wished they could go too.

Mrs Kyndley's husband met them at the door.

The Fat Controller, Thomas' Driver, Fireman, and Guard went upstairs, while the others stood in the sunshine below the window.

The Driver gave her a new dressing-gown to replace the one spoilt by the rain. The Guard brought her some grapes, and the Fireman gave her some woolly slippers, and promised to bring some coal as a present from Thomas,

next time they passed.

Mrs Kyndley was very pleased with her presents.

"You are very good to me," she said.

"The passengers and I," said the Fat Controller, "hope you will accept these tickets for the South Coast, Mrs Kyndley, and get really well in the sunshine. We cannot thank you enough for preventing that accident. I hope we have not tired you. Goodbye and a happy Christmas."

Then going quietly downstairs, they joined the group outside the window, and sang some carols before returning to the train.

Mrs Kyndley is now at Bournemouth, getting better every day, and Thomas and Toby are looking forward to the time when they can welcome her home.

Gordon the Big Engine

THE REV. W. AWDRY

with illustrations by

C. REGINALD DALBY

DEAR IAN,
    You asked for a book about Gordon. Here it is.
Gordon has been naughty, and the Fat Controller was
stern with him.
    Gordon has now learnt his lesson and is a Really
Useful Engine again.

THE AUTHOR

Off the Rails

GORDON was resting in a siding.

"Peep peep! Peep peep! Hullo, Fatface!" whistled Henry.

"What cheek!" spluttered Gordon. "That Henry is too big for his wheels; fancy speaking to me like that! Me e e e e!" he went on, letting off steam, "Me e e e who has never had an accident!"

"Aren't jammed whistles and burst safety valves accidents?" asked Percy innocently.

"No indeed!" said Gordon huffily, "high spirits – might happen to any engine; but to come off the rails, well I ask you! Is it right? Is it decent?"

A few days later it was Henry's turn to take the Express. Gordon watched him getting ready.

"Be careful, Henry," he said, "You're not pulling the 'Flying Kipper' now; mind you keep on the rails today."

Henry snorted away, Gordon yawned and went to sleep.

But he didn't sleep long. "Wake up, Gordon," said his Driver, "a Special train's coming and we're to pull it."

Gordon opened his eyes. "Is it Coaches or Trucks?"

"Trucks," said his Driver.

"Trucks!" said Gordon crossly. "Pah!"

They lit Gordon's fire and oiled him ready for the run. The fire was sulky and wouldn't burn; but they couldn't wait, so Edward pushed him to the turntable to get him facing the right way.

"I *won't* go, I *won't* go," grumbled Gordon.

"Don't be silly, don't be silly," puffed Edward.

Gordon tried hard, but he couldn't stop himself being moved.

At last he was on the turntable, Edward was uncoupled and backed away, and Gordon's Driver and Fireman jumped down to turn him round.

The movement had shaken Gordon's fire; it was now burning nicely and making steam.

Gordon was cross, and didn't care what he did.

He waited till the table was half-way round. "I'll show them! I'll show them!" he hissed, and moved slowly forward.

He only meant to go a little way, just far enough to "jam" the table, and stop it turning, as he had done once before. But

he couldn't stop himself, and, slithering down the embankment, he settled in a ditch.

"Oooosh!" he hissed as his wheels **churned the mud**. "Get me out! Get me out!"

"Not a hope," said his Driver and Fireman, "you're stuck, you **silly** great engine, don't you **understand** that?"

They telephoned the Fat Controller.

"So Gordon didn't want to take the Special and ran into a ditch," he answered from his office. "What's that you say? The Special's waiting – tell Edward to take it please – and Gordon? Oh leave him where he is; we haven't time to bother with him now."

A family of toads croaked crossly at Gordon as he lay in the mud. On the other side of the ditch some little boys were chattering.

"Coo! Doesn't he look silly!"

"They'll never get him out."

They began to sing:

Silly old Gordon fell in a ditch,
fell in a ditch,
fell in a ditch,
Silly old Gordon fell in a ditch,
All on a Monday morning.

The School bell rang and, still singing, they chased down the road.

"Pshaw!" said Gordon, and blew away three tadpoles and an inquisitive newt.

Gordon lay in the ditch all day.

"Oh dear!" he thought, "I shall never get out."

But that evening they brought floodlights; then with powerful jacks they lifted Gordon and made a road of sleepers under his wheels to keep him from the mud.

Strong wire ropes were fastened to his back end, and James and Henry, pulling hard, at last managed to bring him to the rails.

Late that night Gordon crawled home a sadder and a wiser engine!

Leaves

Two men were cleaning Gordon.

"Mind my eye," Gordon grumbled.

"Shut it, silly! Did ever you see such mud, Bert?"

"No I never, Alf! You ought to be ashamed, Gordon, giving us extra work."

The hosing and scrubbing stopped. Gordon opened one eye, but shut it quickly.

"Wake up, Gordon," said the Fat Controller sternly, "and listen to me. You will pull no more coaches till you are a Really Useful Engine."

So Gordon had to spend his time pulling trucks.

"Goods trains, Goods trains," he muttered. He felt his position deeply.

"That's for you! – and *you*! – and *you*!" Gordon said crossly.

"Oh! Oh! Oh! Oh!" screamed the trucks as he shunted them about the Yard.

"Trucks will be trucks," said James, watching him.

"They won't with *me*!" snorted Gordon. "I'll teach them. Go on!" and another truck scurried away.

"They tried to push me down the hill this morning," Gordon explained. "It's slippery there. You'll probably need some help."

"*I* don't need help on hills," said James huffily.

Gordon laughed, and got ready for his next train.

James went away to take the Express.

"Slippery hills indeed," he snorted. "*I* don't need help."

"Come on! Come on!" he puffed.

"All in good time, all in good time," grumbled the coaches.

The train was soon running nicely, but a "Distant" signal checked them close to Gordon's Hill.

Gordon's Hill used to be bleak and bare. Strong winds from the sea made it hard to climb. Trees were planted to give shelter, and in summer the trains run through a leafy avenue.

Now autumn had come, and dead leaves fell. The wind usually puffed them away, but today rain made them heavy, and they did not move.

The "Home" signal showed "clear", and James began to go faster.

He started to climb the hill.

"I'll do it! I'll do it!" he puffed confidently.

Half-way up he was not so sure! "I *must* do it, I *must* do it," he panted desperately, but try as he would, his wheels slipped on the leaves, and he couldn't pull the train at all.

"Whatsthematter? Whatsthematter?" he gasped.

"Steady old boy, steady," soothed his Driver.

His Fireman put sand on the rails to help him grip; but James' wheels spun so fast that they only ground the sand and leaves to slippery mud, making things worse than before.

The train slowly stopped. Then –

"Help! Help! Help!" whistled James; for though his wheels were turning forwards, the heavy coaches pulled him backwards, and the whole train started slipping down the hill.

His Driver shut off steam, carefully put on the brakes, and skillfully stopped the train.

"Whew!" he sat down and mopped his face. "I've never known *that* happen before."

"I have," said the Fireman, "in Bincombe tunnel – Southern Region."

The Guard poked his head in the cab. "Now what?" he asked.

"Back to the station," said the Fireman, taking charge, "and send for a 'Banker'."

So the Guard warned the Signalman, and they brought the train safely down.

But Gordon, who had followed with a goods train, saw what had happened.

Gordon left his trucks, and crossed over to James.

"I thought you could climb hills," he chuckled.

James didn't answer; he had no steam!

"Ah well! We live and learn," said Gordon, "we live and learn. Never mind, little James," he went on kindly, "I'm

going to push behind. Whistle when you're ready."

James waited till he had plenty of steam, then "Peep! Peep!" he called.

"Poop! Poop! Poop!"

"Pull hard," puffed Gordon.

"We'll do it!" puffed James.

"Pull hard! We'll do it," the engines puffed together.

Clouds of smoke and steam towered from the snorting engines as they struggled up the hill.

"We *can* do it!" puffed James.

"We *will* do it!" puffed Gordon.

The greasy rails sometimes made Gordon's wheels slip, but he never gave up, and presently they reached the top.

"We've done it! We've done it!" they puffed.

Gordon stopped. "Poop! Poop! He whistled. "Goodbye."

"Peep! Peep! Peep! Peep! Thank you! Goodbye," answered James. Gordon watched the coaches wistfully till they were out of sight; then slowly he trundled back to his waiting trucks.

Down the Mine

ONE day Thomas was at the junction, when Gordon shuffled in with some trucks.

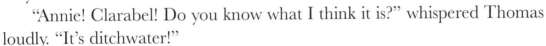

"Poof!" remarked Thomas, "what a funny smell!"

"Can you smell a smell?"

"I can't smell a smell," said Annie and Clarabel.

"A funny, musty sort of smell," said Thomas.

"No one noticed it till you did," grunted Gordon. "It must be yours."

"Annie! Clarabel! Do you know what I think it is?" whispered Thomas loudly. "It's ditchwater!"

Gordon snorted, but before he could answer, Thomas puffed quickly away.

Annie and Clarabel could hardly believe their ears!

"He's *dreadfully* rude; I feel quite ashamed." "I feel *quite* ashamed, he's dreadfully rude," they twittered to each other.

"You mustn't be rude, you make us ashamed," they kept telling Thomas.

But Thomas didn't care a bit.

"That was funny, that was funny," he chuckled. He felt very pleased with himself.

Annie and Clarabel were deeply shocked. They had a great respect for Gordon the Big Engine.

Thomas left the coaches at a station and went to a mine for some trucks.

Long ago, miners, digging for lead, had made tunnels under the ground.

Though strong enough to hold up trucks, their roofs could not bear the weight of engines.

A large notice said: "DANGER, ENGINES MUST NOT PASS THIS BOARD."

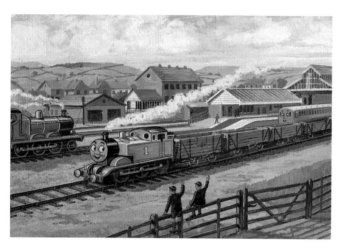

Thomas had often been warned, but he didn't care.

"Silly old board," he thought. He had often tried to pass it, but had never succeeded.

This morning he laughed as he puffed along. He had made a plan.

He had to push empty trucks into one siding, and pull out full ones from another.

His Driver stopped him, and the Fireman went to turn the points.

"Come on," waved the Fireman, and they started.

The Driver leaned out of the cab to see where they were going.

"Now!" said Thomas to himself, and, bumping the trucks fiercely, he jerked his Driver off the footplate.

"Hurrah!" laughed Thomas, and he followed the trucks into the siding.

"Stupid old board!" said Thomas as he passed it. "There's no danger; there's no danger."

His Driver, unhurt, jumped up. "Look out!" he shouted.

The Fireman clambered into the cab. Thomas squealed crossly as his brakes were applied.

"It's quite safe," he hissed.

"Come back," yelled the Driver, but before they could move, there was rumbling and the rails quivered.

The Fireman jumped clear. As he did so the ballast slipped away and the rails sagged and broke.

"Fire and Smoke!" said Thomas, "I'm sunk!" – and he was!

Thomas could just see out of the hole, but he couldn't move.

"Oh dear!" he said, "I am a silly engine."

"And a very naughty one too," said a voice behind him, "I saw you."

"Please get me out; I won't be naughty again."

"I'm not so sure," replied the Fat Controller. "We can't lift you out with a crane, the ground's

not firm enough. Hm . . . Let me see . . . I wonder if Gordon could pull you out."

"Yes Sir," said Thomas nervously. He didn't want to meet Gordon just yet!

"Down a mine is he? Ho! Ho! Ho!" laughed Gordon.

"What a joke! What a joke!" he chortled, puffing to the rescue.

"Poop! Poop! Little Thomas," he whistled, "we'll have you out in a couple of puffs."

Strong cables were fastened between the two engines.

"Poop! Poop! Poop!"

"Are you ready? HEAVE," called the Fat Controller.

But they didn't pull Thomas out in two puffs; Gordon was panting hard and nearly purple before he had dragged Thomas out of the hold, and safely past the board.

"I'm sorry I was cheeky," said Thomas.

"That's all right, Thomas. You made me laugh. I like that. I'm in disgrace," Gordon went on pathetically, "I feel very low."

"I'm in disgrace too," said Thomas.

"Why! so you are Thomas; we're both in disgrace. Shall we form an Alliance?"

"An Ally – what – was – it?"

"An Alliance, Thomas, 'United we stand, together we fall'," said Gordon grandly.

"You help me, and I help you. How about it?"

"Right you are," said Thomas.

"Good! That's settled," rumbled Gordon.

And buffer to buffer the Allies puffed home.

Paint Pots and Queens

THE stations on the line were being painted.

The engines were surprised.

"The Queen is coming," said the painters. The engines in their Shed were excited and wondered who would pull the Royal Train.

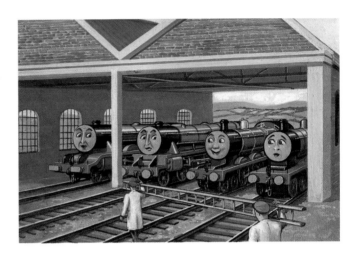

"I'm too old to pull important trains," said Edward sadly.

"I'm in disgrace," Gordon said gloomily. "The Fat Controller would never choose me."

"He'll choose me, of course," boasted James the Red Engine.

"You!" Henry snorted, "*You* can't climb hills. He will ask *me* to pull it, *and* I'll have a new coat of paint. You wait and see."

The days passed. Henry puffed about proudly, quite sure that he would be the Royal Engine.

One day when it rained, his Driver and Fireman stretched a tarpaulin from the cab to the tender, to keep themselves dry.

Henry puffed into the Big Station. A painter was climbing a ladder above the line. Henry's smoke puffed upwards; it was thick and black. The painter choked and couldn't see. He missed his footing on the ladder, dropped his paint pot, and fell plop on to Henry's tarpaulin.

The paint poured over Henry's boiler, and trickled down each side. The paint pot perched on his dome.

The painter clambered down and shook his brush at Henry.

"You spoil my clean paint with your dirty smoke," he said, "and then you take the whole lot, and make me go and fetch some more." He stumped crossly away.

The Fat Controller pushed through the crowd.

"You look like an iced cake, Henry," he said. "*That* won't do for the Royal Train. I must make other arrangements."

He walked over to the Yard.

Gordon and Thomas saw him coming, and both began to speak.

"Please Sir ———"

"One at a time," smiled the Fat Controller. "Yes Gordon?"

"May Thomas have his Branch Line again?"

"Hm," said the Fat Controller, "well Thomas?"

"Please, Sir, can Gordon pull coaches now?"

The Fat Controller pondered.

"Hm ——— you've both been quite good lately, and you deserve a treat ——— When the Queen comes, Edward will go in front and clear the line, Thomas will look after the coaches, and Gordon ——— will pull the train."

"Ooooh Sir!" said the engines happily.

The great day came. Percy, Toby, Henry and James worked hard bringing people to the town.

Thomas sorted all their coaches in the Yard.

"Peep! Peep! Peep! They're coming!" Edward steamed in, looking smart with flags and bright paint.

Two minutes passed – five – seven – ten. "Poop! Poop!" Everyone knew that whistle, and a mighty cheer went up as the Queen's train glided into the station.

Gordon was spotless, and his brass shone. Like Edward, he was decorated with flags, but on his buffer beam he proudly carried the Royal Arms.

The Queen was met by the Fat Controller, and before doing anything else, she thanked him for their splendid run.

"Not at all, Your Majesty," he said, "thank *you*."

"We have read," said the Queen to the Fat Controller, "a great deal about your engines. May we see them please?"

So he led the way to where all the engines were waiting.

"Peep! Peep!" whistled Toby and Percy, "they're coming!"

"Sh Sh! Sh Sh!" hissed Henry and James.

But Toby and Percy were too excited to care.

The Fat Controller told the Queen their names, and she talked to each engine. Then she turned to go.

Percy bubbled over, "Three cheers for the Queen!" he called.

"Peeeep! Peeeep! Peeeep!" whistled all the engines.

The Fat Controller held his ears, but the Queen, smiling, waved to the engines till she passed the gate.

Next day the Queen spoke specially to Thomas, who fetched her coaches,

and to Edward and Gordon who took her away; and no engines ever felt prouder than Thomas, and Edward, and Gordon the Big Engine.

THE RAILWAY SERIES NO. 12

The Eight Famous Engines

THE REV. W. AWDRY

with illustrations by

JOHN T. KENNEY

DEAR FRIENDS,

The Fat Controller's engines are now quite famous.
They have been on the Wireless, and had many other
adventures. But he had another plan too for his
engines, and this book will tell you what it was.

THE AUTHOR

Percy takes the Plunge

SOMETIMES Percy takes stone trucks to the other end of the line. There, he meets engines from the Other Railway.

One day, Henry wanted to rest in the Shed; but Percy was talking to some tank engines.

". . . It was raining hard. Water swirled under my boiler. I couldn't see where I was going; but I struggled on."

"Ooooh Percy, you *are* brave."

"Well," said Percy modestly, "it wasn't anything really. Water's nothing to an engine with determination."

"Tell us more, Percy," said the engines.

"What are you engines doing here?" hissed Henry. "This shed is for the Fat Controller's Engines. Go away."

"Silly things," Henry snorted.

"They're not silly." Percy had been enjoying himself. He was cross because Henry had sent them away.

"They are silly, and so are you. 'Water's nothing to an engine with determination.' Pah!"

"Anyway," said cheeky

Percy, "I'm not afraid of water. I like it." He ran away singing,

"Once an engine attached to a train
Was afraid of a few drops of rain . . ."

Percy arrived home feeling pleased with himself. "Silly old Henry," he chuckled.

Thomas was looking at a board on the Quay. It said "DANGER".

"We mustn't go past it," he said. "That's Orders."

"Why?"

" 'DANGER' means falling down something," said Thomas. "I went past 'DANGER' once, and fell down a mine."

Percy looked beyond the board. "I can't see a mine," he said.

He didn't know that the foundations of the Quay had sunk, and that the rails now sloped downward to the sea.

"Stupid board!" said Percy. For days and days he tried to sidle past it; but his Driver stopped him every time.

"No you don't," he would say.

Then Percy made a plan. One day at the Top Station he whispered to the trucks. "Will you give me a bump when we get to the Quay?"

The trucks were surprised. They had never been asked to bump an engine before. They giggled and chattered about it the whole way down.

"Whoah Percy! Whoah!" said his Driver, and Percy checked obediently at the "distant" signal.

"Driver doesn't know my plan," he chuckled.

"On! On! On!" laughed the trucks. Percy thought they were helping. "I'll pretend to stop at the station; but the trucks will push me past the board. Then I'll make them stop. I can do that whenever I like."

If Percy hadn't been so conceited, he would never have been so silly.

Every wise engine knows that you cannot trust trucks.

They reached the station, and Percy's brakes groaned. That was the signal for the trucks.

"Go on! Go on!" they yelled, and surged forward together.

They gave Percy a fearful bump, and knocked his Driver and Fireman off the footplate.

"Ow!" said Percy, sliding past the board.

The day was misty. The rails were slippery. His wheels wouldn't grip.

Percy was frantic. "That's enough!" he hissed.

But it was too late. Once on the slope, he tobogganed helplessly down, crashed through

the buffers, and slithered into the sea.

"You are a very disobedient engine."

Percy knew that voice. He groaned.

The Foreman borrowed a small boat and rowed the Fat Controller round.

"Please, Sir, get me out Sir, I'm truly sorry Sir."

"No, Percy, we cannot do that till high tide. I hope it will teach you to obey Orders."

"Yes, Sir," Percy shivered miserably. He was cold. Fish were playing hide and seek through his wheels. The tide rose higher and higher.

He was feeling his position more and more deeply every minute.

It was nearly dark when they brought floating cranes, cleared away the trucks, and lifted Percy out.

He was too cold and stiff to move by himself, so he was sent to the Works next day on Henry's goods train.

"Well! Well! Well!" chuckled Henry, "Did you like the water?"

"No."

"I *am* surprised. You need more determination, Percy. 'Water's nothing to an engine with determination' you know. Perhaps you will like it better next time."

But Percy is quite determined that there won't be a "next time".

Gordon goes Foreign

LOTS of people travel to the Big Station at the end of the line. Engines from the Other Railway sometimes pull their trains. These engines stay the night and go home next day.

Gordon was talking one day to one of these.

"When I was young and green," he said, "I remember going to London. Do you know the place? The station's called King's Cross."

"King's Cross!" snorted the engine, "London's Euston. Everybody knows that."

"Rubbish!" said Duck, "London's Paddington. I *know*. I worked there."

They argued till they went to sleep. They argued when they woke up. They were still arguing when the other engine went away.

"Stupid thing," said Gordon crossly, "I've no patience."

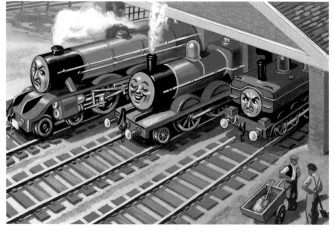

"Stupid yourself," said Duck, "London's Paddington, PADDINGTON, do you hear?"

"Stop arguing," James broke in, "you make me tired. You're both agreed about something anyway."

"What's that?"

"London's not Euston," laughed James. "Now shut up!"

Gordon rolled away still grumbling. "I'm sure it's King's Cross. I'll go and prove it."

But that was easier said than done.

London lay beyond the Big Station at the other end of the Line. Gordon had to stop there. Another engine then took his train.

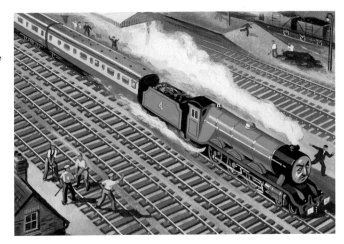

"If I didn't stop," he thought, "I could go to London."

One day he ran right through the station. Another time he tried to start before the Fireman could uncouple the coaches. He tried all sorts of tricks; but it was no good. His Driver checked him every time.

"Oh dear!" he thought sadly, "I'll never get there."

One day he pulled the Express to the station as usual. His Fireman

uncoupled the coaches, and he ran on to his siding to wait till it was time to go home.

The coaches waited and waited at the platform; but their engine didn't come.

A porter ran across and spoke to Gordon's Driver. "The Inspector's on the platform. He wants to see you."

The Driver climbed down from the cab and walked over the station. He came back in a few minutes looking excited.

"Hullo!" said the Fireman, "what's happened?"

"The engine for the Express turned over when it was coming out of the Yard. Nothing else can come in or out. They want us to take the train to London. I said we would, if the Fat Controller agreed. They telephoned, and he said we could do it. How's that?"

"Fine," said the Fireman, "we'll show them what the Fat Controller's

engines can do."

"Come on!" said Gordon, "let's go." He rolled quickly over the crossings and backed on to the train.

It was only a few minutes before the Guard blew his whistle; but Gordon thought it was ages!

"COME ON! COME ON!" he puffed to the coaches.

"Comeoncomeoncomeon!"

"We're going to Town, we're going to Town," sang the coaches slowly at first, then faster and faster.

Gordon found that London was a long way away. "Never mind," he said, "I like a good long run to stretch my wheels."

But all the same he was glad when London came in sight.

The Fat Controller came into his office next morning. He looked at the letters on his desk. One had a London post-mark.

"I wonder how Gordon's getting on," he said.

The Stationmaster knocked and came in. He looked excited.

"Excuse me Sir, have you seen the news?"

"Not yet. Why?"

"Just look at this Sir."

The Fat Controller took the

Newspaper. "Good gracious me!" he said, "there's Gordon. Headlines too! 'FAMOUS ENGINE AT LONDON STATION. POLICE CALLED TO CONTROL CROWDS.'"

The Fat Controller read on, absorbed.

Gordon returned next day. The Fat Controller spoke to his Driver and Fireman. "I see you had a good welcome in London."

"We certainly did Sir! We signed autographs till our arms ached, and Gordon had his photograph taken from so many directions at once that he didn't know which way to look!"

"Good!" smiled the Fat Controller, "I expect he enjoyed himself. Didn't you Gordon?"

"No Sir, I didn't."

"Why ever not?"

"London's all wrong," answered Gordon sadly, "they've changed it. It isn't King's Cross any more. It's St Pancras."

Double Header

THE Fat Controller gave Gordon a rest when he came back from London. He told James to do his work.

James got very conceited about it.

"You know, little Toby," he said one day, "I'm an Important Engine now; everybody knows it. They come in crowds to see me flash by. The heaviest train makes no difference. I'm as regular as clockwork. They all set their watches by me. Never late, always on time, that's me."

"Sez you," replied Toby cheekily.

Toby was out on the Main Line. The Fat Controller had sent him to the Works. His parts were worn. They clanked as he trundled along.

He was enjoying his journey. He was a little engine, and his tanks didn't hold much water, so he often had to stop for a drink. He had small wheels, too, and he couldn't go fast.

"Never mind," he thought, "the Signalmen all know me; they'll give me plenty of time."

But a new Signalman had come to one of the stations.

Toby had wanted to take Henrietta, but the Fat Controller had said, "No! What would the passengers do without her?"

He wondered if Henrietta was lonely. Percy had promised to look after her; but Toby couldn't help worrying. "Percy doesn't understand her like I do," he said.

He felt thirsty and tired; he had come a long way.

He saw a "distant" signal. "Good," he thought, "now I can have a nice drink, and rest in a siding till James has gone by."

Toby's Driver thought so too. They stopped by the water-crane. His Fireman jumped out and put the hose in his tank.

Toby was enjoying his drink when the Signalman came up. Toby had never seen him before.

"No time for that," said the Signalman. "We must clear the road for the Express."

"Right," said the Driver. "We'll wait in the siding."

"No good," said the Signalman, "it's full of trucks. You'll have to hurry to the next

station. They've got plenty of room for you there."

Poor Toby clanked sadly away. "I must hurry! I must hurry!" he panted.

But hurrying used a lot of water, and his tanks were soon empty.

They damped down his fire and struggled on, but he soon ran out of steam, and stood marooned on the Main Line far away from the next station.

The Fireman walked back. He put detonators on the line to warn James and his Driver; then he hurried along the sleepers.

"I'll tell that Signalman something," he said grimly.

James was fuming when Toby's Fireman arrived and explained what had happened.

"My fault," said the Signalman, "I didn't understand about Toby."

"Now James," said his Driver, "you'll have to push him."

"What, me?" snorted James. "ME, push Toby *and* pull my train?"

"Yes, you."

"Shan't."

The Driver, the Firemen, the passengers and the Guard all said he was a Bad Engine.

"All right, all right," grumbled James. He came up behind Toby and gave him a bump.

"Get on you!" he said crossly.

James' Driver made him push Toby all the way to the Works. "It serves you right for being cross," he said.

James had to work very hard and when he reached the Works Station he felt exhausted.

Some little boys ran along the platform. "Coo!" said one, "The Express *is* late. A double header too. Do you know what I think? I think," he went on, "that James couldn't pull the train, so Toby had to help him."

"Cor!" said James and disappeared in a cloud of steam.

The Fat Controller's Engines

ONE evening, Thomas brought his last train to the junction. He went for a drink.

"I'm going to the Big Station," he said to Percy and Toby.

"So are we," they answered.

"Do you know," Percy went on, "I think something's up." Toby looked at the sky, "Where?"

"Down here, silly," laughed Thomas.

"How," asked Toby reasonably, "can something be up when it's down?"

"Look!" said Thomas excitedly, "Look!"

Seven engines from the Other Railway were coming along the line.

"Hullo Jinty!" whistled Percy, "Hullo Pug!

"They're friends of mine," he explained. "I don't know the others."

Jinty and Pug whistled cheerfully as they puffed though the station.

"What *is* all this?" asked Thomas.

"The Fat Controller's got a plan," answered his Driver, "and he's going to tell it to us. Come on."

So they followed to the Big Station at the end of the line where all the engines had gone.

The Fat Controller was waiting for them there.

"The people of England," he said, "read about Us in the Books; but they do not think that we are real. . . ."

"Shame!" squeaked Percy. The Fat Controller glared. Percy subsided.

". . . so," he continued, "I am taking My Engines to England to show them."

"Hooray! Hooray!" the engines whistled.

The Fat Controller held his ears. "Silence!" he bellowed.

"We start the day after tomorrow at 8 a.m. Meanwhile as these engines have kindly come from the Other Railway to take your place, you will show them your work tomorrow."

Next day, as Annie and Clarabel were going to England too, Thomas and Jinty practised with some other coaches.

Thomas was excited. He began boasting about his race with Bertie. "I whooshed through the tunnel and stopped an inch from the buffers. Like this!"

—— CRASH — The buffers broke.

No one was hurt; but Thomas' front was badly bent.

They telephoned the Fat Controller. "I'll send up some men," he said, "but if they can't mend Thomas in time, we'll go to England without him."

Next morning the engines waited at the junction. Toby and Percy were each on a truck and Duck had pushed them into place behind Edward.

Henrietta stood on a siding. The Fat Controller had called her a "curiosity". "I wouldn't dream of leaving you behind," he said, "I'll fit you up

as my private coach." She felt very grand.

Gordon, James and Henry were in front. They whistled impatiently.

The Fat Controller paced the platform. He looked at his watch. "One minute more," he said, turning to the Guard.

"Peep peep peeep!" whistled Thomas and panted into the station.

Annie and Clarabel twittered anxiously. "We hope we're not late; it isn't quite Eight."

"Thomas," said the Fat Controller sternly, "I am most displeased with you. You nearly upset My Arrangements."

Thomas, abashed, arranged himself and the coaches behind Duck, without saying a word!

The Fat Controller climbed into Henrietta. The Guard blew his whistle and waved his flag.

The engines whistled, "Look out England, here we come!" and the cavalcade puffed off.

The engines stood side by side in a big airy shed. Hundreds of people came to see them, and climbed in and out of their cabs every day.

They liked it at first, but

presently felt very bored, and were glad when it was time to go.

The people along their line put the flags out, and cheered them home. "We are glad to see you," they said. "Those others did their best; but they don't know our ways. Nothing anywhere can compare with our Fat Controller's engines."

Afterword
BY BRIAN SIBLEY
The Thomas the Tank Engine Man:
The Reverend W. Awdry

Wilbert Awdry with an engine from the Dean Forest Railway.

THE man who was to create Thomas the Tank Engine and the other characters in the famous *Railway Series* was born on 15 June 1911, the son of the Reverend Vere Awdry, vicar of Ampfield, near Romsey in Hampshire. He was christened Wilbert Vere Awdry (his first name combining those of his father's favourite brothers, William and Herbert) and inherited a passion for steam engines which had led his father to build a model railway layout in the vicarage garden. Wilbert's father used to take him on walks around the parish during which they often met and talked with local railwaymen; and, long before he could read, Wilbert would sit poring over the pictures in his father's bound copies of *The Railway Magazine*.

A brother, George, was born when Wilbert was five and, soon afterwards, the Awdry family moved to Box in Wiltshire, near the Great Western Railway's main line from Paddington to Bristol. It was here that the seeds of the *Railway Series* were sown.

Lying in bed as a child I would hear a heavy goods train coming in and stopping at Box station, then the three whistles, crowing for a banker, a tank-engine, which would come out of his little shed to help the goods train up the gradient. There was no doubt in my mind that steam engines all had definite personalities. I would hear them snorting up the grade and little imagination was needed to hear in the puffings and pantings of the two engines the conversation they were having with one another: 'I can't do it! I can't do it! I can't do it!' 'Yes, you can! Yes, you can! Yes, you can!'

Wilbert was educated at Dauntsey School in West Lavington, Wiltshire, before going to St Peter's Hall, Oxford, where he gained his BA and MA. Deciding to go into the ministry of the Church of England, Wilbert studied theology at Wycliffe Hall and, before being ordained, worked as a teacher at St George's School in Jerusalem. It was there that he met and became engaged to Margaret Emily Wale, a teacher at the English High School in Haifa.

Returning to England, Wilbert was ordained deacon at Winchester Cathedral in December 1936 and became a curate at Odiham in Hampshire. Marrying Margaret when she returned from the Holy Land in 1938, Wilbert moved to West Lavington in Wiltshire, as curate to the clergyman who had once been his school chaplain. Problems arose in 1939, when – as war in Europe became an inevitability – Wilbert declared himself a pacifist. He was asked to leave the parish and was on the point of giving up his work as a priest when the pacifist Bishop of Birmingham appointed him to a curacy at the parish of King's Norton.

It was in Birmingham, in 1940, that Wilbert and Margaret's first child, Christopher, was born, followed by two daughters, Veronica in 1943 and Hilary in 1946. When Christopher was two years old he was confined to bed with measles. Wilbert entertained his son with a story about a little old engine who was sad.

'Why is he sad, Daddy?'
'Because he's old and hasn't been out for a long time.'
'What's his name, Daddy?'
'Edward!'

It was the first name that came into Wilbert's head. By question and answer, he invented the Cinderella-type story of 'Edward's Day Out': how the little engine was eventually given the chance to take out a train of his own.

The story was told over and over again and was eventually written down and illustrated with simple line drawings. The adventures of Edward – along with two other engines, Gordon and Henry – might easily have been forgotten had not Margaret Awdry encouraged her husband to offer them to a publisher.

In 1945, after being turned down by several publishers, the book was accepted by Edmund Ward and published as *The Three Railway Engines*.

The master storyteller and a young admirer at a model railway exhibition.

The most famous of all Wilbert Awdry's engine characters appeared the following year in *Thomas the Tank Engine*.

In 1946, Wilbert was given his first parish at Elsworth and Knapwell, near Cambridge, where he stayed for seven years before moving to Emneth, near Wisbech. During these years, Wilbert continued writing books for children and from *James the Red Engine* in 1948, published a new *Railway Series* title each year until his last book, *Tramway Engines*, in 1972. The stories featured the already established engines, Thomas, Edward, Gordon and Henry, as well as introducing new characters in such volumes as *Toby the Tram Engine*, *Percy the Small Engine* and *Duck and the Diesel Engine* which featured the type of disagreeable non-steam engine that were increasingly taking over from traditional locomotives to the disgust of Wilbert Awdry and many other steam enthusiasts.

With his brother, George, Wilbert invented a fictional setting for his stories situated between the British mainland and the Isle of Man and called the Island of Sodor. The Awdry brothers made maps and wrote a long, detailed history of the island, its people and railway engines which helped shape many of the events described in the later volumes of the series.

Wilbert also pursued other railway interests: building ambitious model railway layouts in each of his vicarages, taking railway excursions at home and abroad with his brother or his friend the Reverend 'Teddy' Boston, and becoming involved with the work of various railway preservation societies, such as the Talyllyn Railway in Wales, which was to inspire the Skarloey Railway on the Island of Sodor, featured in such books as *Four Little Engines* and *The Little Old Engine*.

Another preserved railway was to honour the author of the *Railway Series* when, in 1987, the Dean Forest Railway named one of its engines 'Wilbert'. By this time, however, Wilbert Awdry had long ceased to be a full-time

clergyman. In 1965, he had retired, or as he puts it, gone 'into private practice', and moved with his wife to Stroud in Gloucestershire. Sadly, Margaret Awdry died in 1989, the year after she and Wilbert celebrated their Golden Wedding Anniversary.

In addition to the *Railway Series*, Wilbert Awdry wrote two children's novels about the adventures of a little red three-wheeled car, *Belinda the Beetle* and *Belinda Beats the Band*, and co-edited and contributed to several adult books about railways.

In 1983, eleven years after Wilbert Awdry wrote his last *Railway Series* title, his son, Christopher, published *Really Useful Engines*, the first of, to date, fourteen books about the engines of Sodor. The book, like its successors, was illustrated by Clive Spong who – like Reginald Dalby and John Kenney before him – studied at Leicester College of Art. The following year, 1984, saw the premiere of Britt Allcroft's popular TV series, *Thomas the Tank Engine and Friends*, narrated by Ringo Starr.

The fiftieth anniversary of the first publication of *The Three Railway Engines* was celebrated in 1995 with an exhibition at the National Railway Museum in York. An InterCity 225, running on the East Coast line between London and Glasgow, was named the 'Reverend W. Awdry' and the same day saw the publication of a biography, *The Thomas the Tank Engine Man*. In recognition of his services to children's literarture, Wilbert Awdry was awarded an O.B.E. in the 1996 New Years Honours List.

In his later years, Mr Awdry suffered from osteoporosis, but despite becoming increasingly bed-ridden, he managed, nevertheless, to reply to the voluminous correspondence he received from Thomas fans all over the world.

After a prolonged illness, Wilbert Awdry died peacefully, aged 85, on 21 March 1997, at his home in Stroud.

Acknowledgements:
Brian Sibley for permission to use material previously published in *The Thomas the Tank Engine Man*
(Heinemann 1995) in the Afterword section of this book; Brighton Evening Argus (jacket-flap photograph);
The Gloucester Citizen (photograph, page 105); Swindon Evening Advertiser (photograph, page 107).